Dear Parent:
Your child's love of reading starts here!

Every child learns to read in a different way and at his or her own speed. Some go back and forth between reading levels and read favorite books again and again. Others read through each level in order. You can help your young reader improve and become more confident by encouraging his or her own interests and abilities. From books your child reads with you to the first books he or she reads alone, there are I Can Read Books for every stage of reading:

SHARED READING
Basic language, word repetition, and whimsical illustrations, ideal for sharing with your emergent reader

BEGINNING READING
Short sentences, familiar words, and simple concepts for children eager to read on their own

READING WITH HELP
Engaging stories, longer sentences, and language play for developing readers

READING ALONE
Complex plots, challenging vocabulary, and high-interest topics for the independent reader

ADVANCED READING
Short paragraphs, chapters, and exciting themes for the perfect bridge to chapter books

I Can Read Books have introduced children to the joy of reading since 1957. Featuring award-winning authors and illustrators and a fabulous cast of beloved characters, I Can Read Books set the standard for beginning readers.

A lifetime of discovery begins with the magical words "I Can Read!"

Visit www.icanread.com for information
on enriching your child's reading experience.

I Can Read!

READING 2 WITH HELP

DREAMWORKS

KUNG FU PANDA ™

Po's Crash Course

HarperCollins®, 🐾®, and I Can Read Book® are trademarks of HarperCollins Publishers.

Kung Fu Panda: Po's Crash Course
Kung Fu Panda ™ & © 2008 DreamWorks Animation L.L.C.
Printed in the United States of America.

Library of Congress catalog card number: 2007936700
ISBN 978-0-06-143461-7
Book design by Rick Farley
❖
First Edition

Po's Crash Course

Adapted by Catherine Hapka

Pencils by Charles Grosvenor

Color by Lydia Halverson

HarperCollins*Publishers*

Po couldn't believe it.
Master Oogway chose him
to be the Dragon Warrior!

He would save the Valley of Peace
with his kung fu moves.
"Woohoo! I'm the guy!"
Po said happily.

The big, awkward panda

was ready to begin his training.

He entered the Jade Palace.

It was just as amazing inside

as he'd always imagined.

"Check it out!" said Po.

"The Trident of Destiny!

And the Urn of Whispering Warriors!"

Then someone came in.

Po recognized him right away.

"Master Shifu!" he said in awe.

Shifu was the trainer
of the Furious Five.
They were the greatest
kung fu warriors
in the Valley of Peace.

Po was so surprised to see Shifu

that he bumped into the Urn.

Crash!

"Do you have some glue?"

Po asked Shifu sheepishly.

Shifu couldn't believe it.

How could Oogway expect him
to train this pudgy, clumsy panda?

"Oogway may have picked you,"
Shifu said to Po,
"but when I'm through with you,
you're going to wish he hadn't."

Po didn't like the sound of that.

But he was not going to be scared off.

He was the Dragon Warrior!

Po followed Shifu

to the training room.

The Five were practicing their moves.

Po decided to show them

some of his own moves.

Pow!

He hit the training dummy.

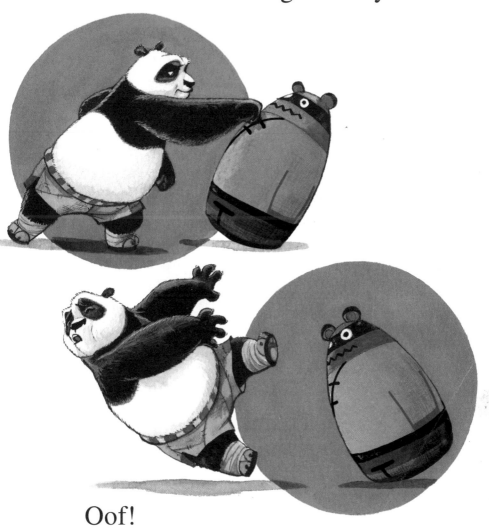

Oof!

The dummy hit him back.

Po kept trying his best.

He stumbled through

the obstacle course.

A spiky ball sent him flying.

He stumbled through a wooden maze,
then found himself dancing around
to avoid shooting flames.
Kung fu was harder than he thought!

That night Po went into
the warriors' bunkhouse.
He was tired from the long day
of training to be the Dragon Warrior.

He tried to be quiet

and not disturb the Five.

But the floor broke under him.

Crack!

He woke up Crane.

"I'm a fan of yours," Po told Crane.

"You guys were awesome at

the Battle of Weeping River!"

"Thanks," Crane said with a yawn.

"You were outnumbered

a thousand to one!" Po said in awe.

He did a kick like one of Crane's.

His foot went through the wall!

"Sorry about that," he said.

Then Po woke up Tigress.

She gave him an angry look.

How could Oogway choose

this goofy panda

as the Dragon Warrior?

"You don't belong here,"
she growled at Po.
"You are a disgrace to kung fu."

In the morning,

Shifu and the Five gathered

outside the training hall.

There was no sign of Po.

Had he already given up?

No way!

Po was inside, training.

There was just one problem.

He had tried a tough kung fu pose.

And now he was stuck!

The Five saw that Po

would keep trying to master kung fu.

They decided to help him train.

At first he didn't do very well.

Po couldn't break the board
that Monkey held up.
So the others all helped him.
At last he broke the board
with his face!

The Five were impressed
with Po's progress.
That night they found him
in the kitchen making soup.

At first Po didn't want

to let them taste the soup.

But they used their kung fu moves

to get the bowl away from him.

The soup was fantastic!

It seemed the bumbling panda
had some hidden talents after all.
Maybe that meant that Oogway
knew exactly what he was doing
when he named Po the Dragon Warrior.